Usborne

First Sticker Book

Building Sites

Illustrated by Stefano Tognetti

Contents

You'll find all the stickers
at the back of the book.

Words by
Jessica Greenwell

Designed by
Yasmin Faulkner

With expert advice on building
sites from Simon Richards.

Starting to build

These workers are getting ready to build new houses. Stick on lots more workers and all their trucks, diggers and tools.

Building a house

Can you help these busy builders with their work?
Give the house a front door and finish its roof.

At the playground

Today the builders are making a new playground at the park.
Stick on the final piece of the climbing frame and a big slide.

Making a bridge

Can you find a section of road to finish this new bridge? Then stick on a tall crane truck.

Road repairs

The builders need to work fast to repair this road.

Add a builders' truck and an excavator to help them.

In the city

New shops and offices are being built in the city.
Stick on everything these builders need to finish the job.

Building tower blocks

To build really tall buildings like these, workers use huge cranes and drilling machines. Add them all to the picture.

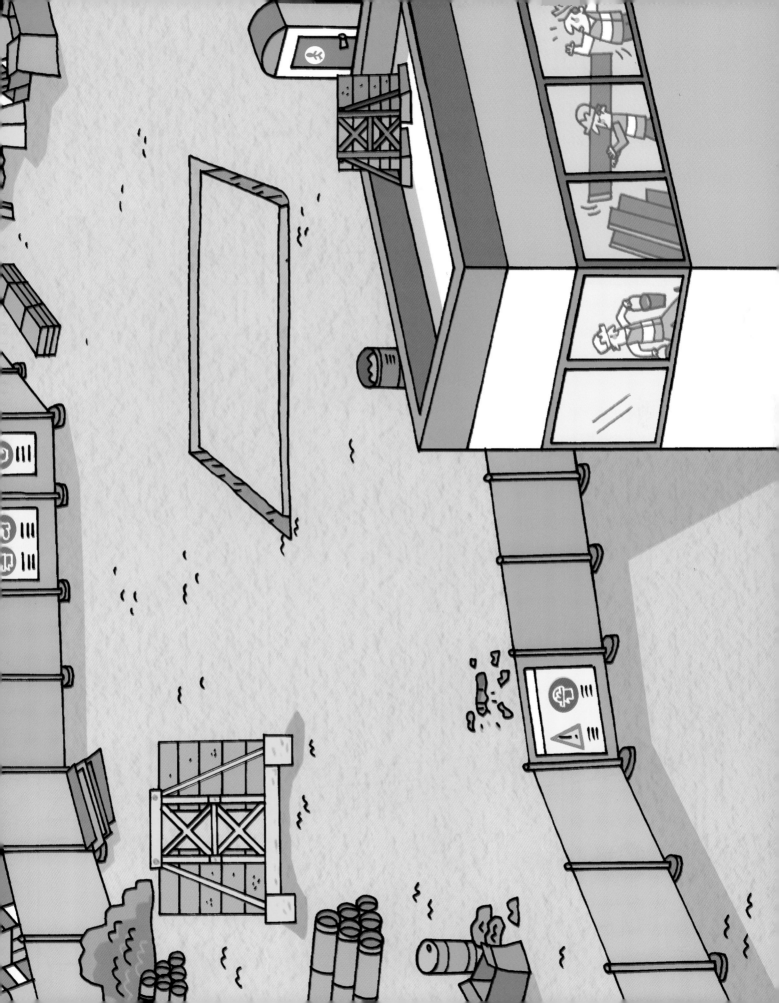

At the demolition site

Add three tracked excavators to the picture – they're pulling this building down with a creak, a rumble and a CRASH!

CAUTION

Make your own picture

Use the stickers to make your own busy building site.

Concrete mixer
truck

Pipes

Load of bricks

Waste
container

Tracked
excavators

Worker directing excavator

Mini dump trucks

Front loader
with claw

Articulated dump truck

Girders

Building a house pages 4–5

Load of bricks

Roof panel

Workers digging

Workers carrying planks

Front porch

Workers carrying a window

Worker climbing a ladder

Worker with cement mixer

Waste container

Skid steer

Worker with wheelbarrow

Builders' truck

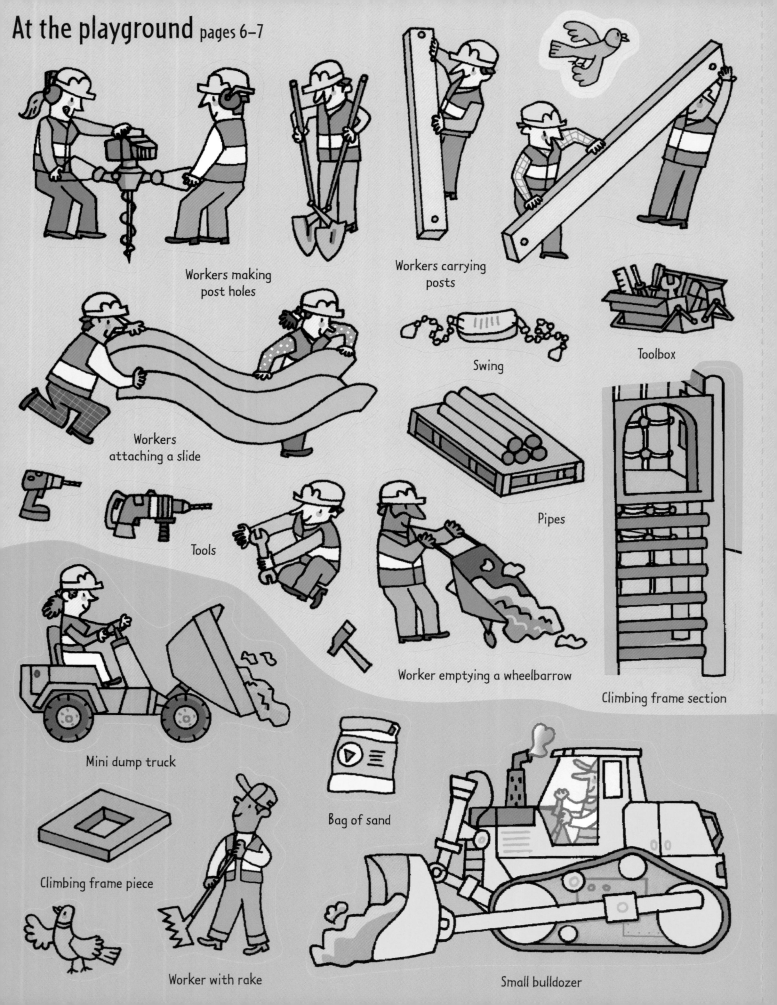

At the playground pages 6–7

Workers making
post holes

Workers carrying
posts

Workers
attaching a slide

Swing

Toolbox

Tools

Pipes

Worker emptying a wheelbarrow

Climbing frame section

Mini dump truck

Climbing frame piece

Bag of sand

Worker with rake

Small bulldozer

Making a bridge page 8

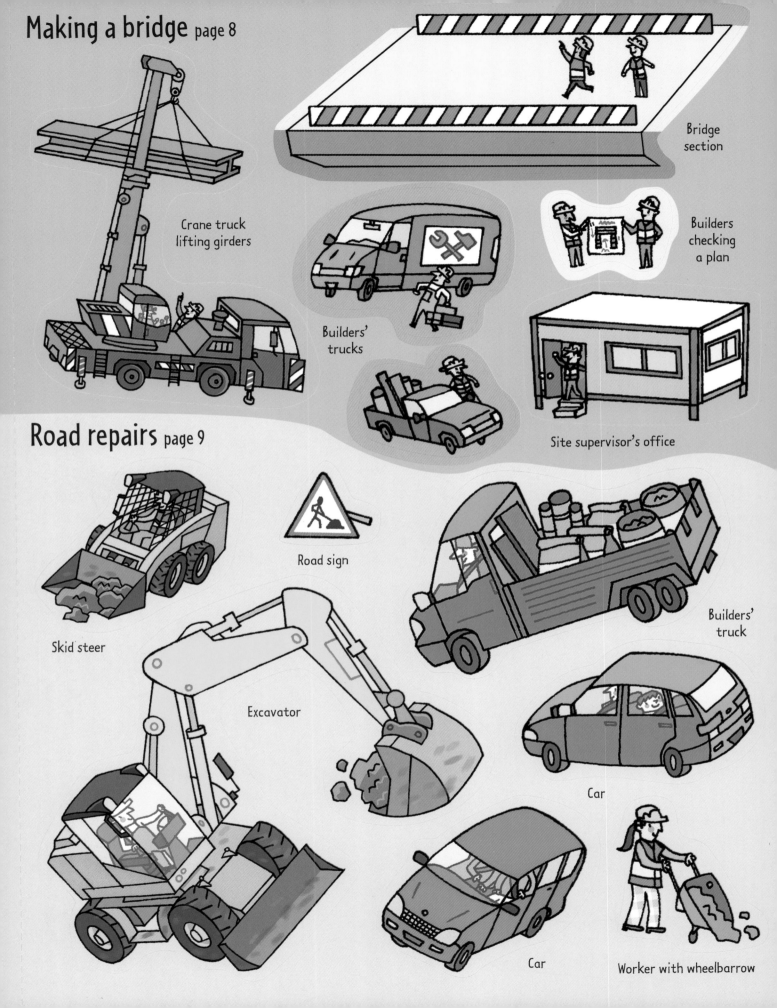

Bridge section

Crane truck lifting girders

Builders' trucks

Builders checking a plan

Site supervisor's office

Road repairs page 9

Skid steer

Road sign

Builders' truck

Excavator

Car

Car

Worker with wheelbarrow

In the city pages 10–11

Window

Workers on scaffolding

Road grader

Pipes

Workers carrying a paving stone

Crane truck

Spirit level

Crates

Mini excavator

Cone

Workers carrying a pipe

Front loader

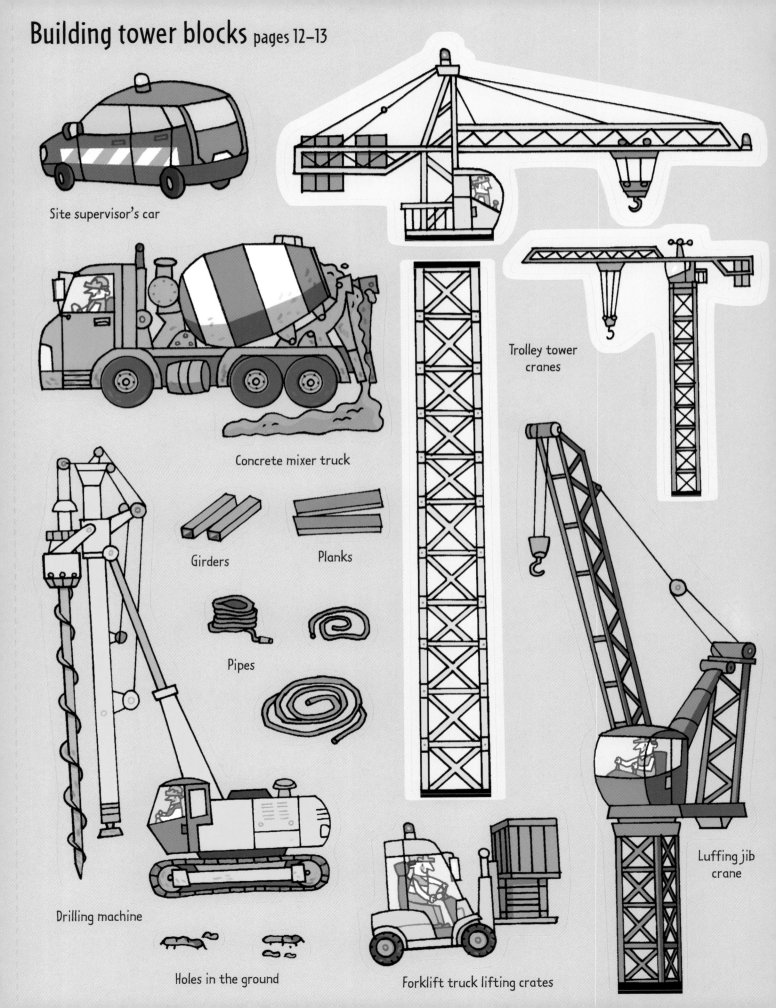

Building tower blocks pages 12–13

Site supervisor's car

Concrete mixer truck

Girders

Planks

Pipes

Drilling machine

Holes in the ground

Trolley tower cranes

Luffing jib crane

Forklift truck lifting crates

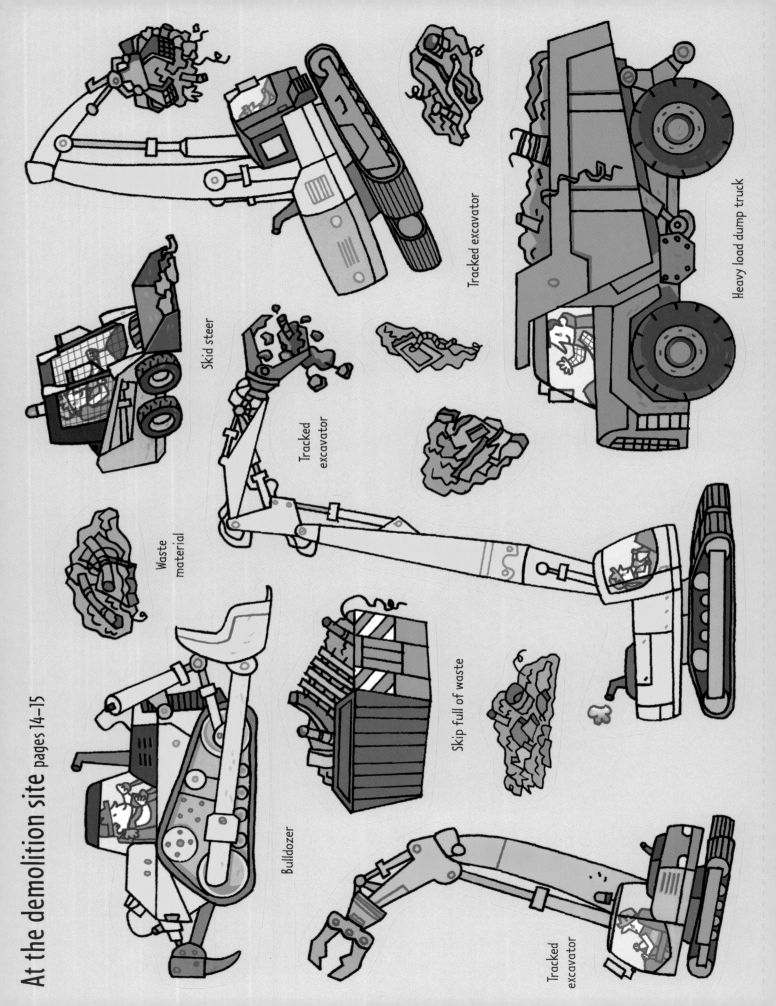

At the demolition site pages 14–15

Tracked excavator

Heavy load dump truck

Skid steer

Tracked excavator

Waste material

Skip full of waste

Bulldozer

Tracked excavator

Make your own picture page 16

Crane truck

Builders' sand

Heavy load dump truck

Mini dump trucks

Skid steer

Front loader
with backhoe

Tracked
excavator

Cones

Worker with shovel

Front loader with backhoe

Worker digging a hole

Builders' sand

Bulldozer